For Sam, Helen, and William D. B.

For Aki, Jeannie, Neelam and Dave Onion M. M.

Text copyright © Sam Williams 2005

Illustration copyright © Mique Moriuchi 2005

First published in the United Kingdom in 2005

by Hodder Children's Books, a division of Hodder Headline Limited

338 Euston Road, London, NW1 3BH

First published in the United States of America

by Holiday House, Inc. in 2005

Printed in Hong Kong

www.holidayhouse.com

First Edition

1 3 5 7 9 10 8 6 4 2

Library of Congress Cataloging-in-Publication Data

Williams, Sam, 1955–

Talk peace / by Sam Williams ; illustrated by Mique Moriuchi.—1st ed.

p. cm.

Summary: Illustrations and easy-to-read text call for all people of the world, wherever they are and whatever they are doing, to talk peace.

ISBN 0-8234-1936-3

[1. Peace—Fiction. 2. Toleration—Fiction.]

I. Moriuchi, Mique, ill. II. Title.

PZ7.W66817535Tal 2005

[E]—dc22

2004055256

Talk Peace

by Sam Williams

illustrated by Mique Moriuchi

Holiday House / New York

Talk
soft.

Talk
loud.

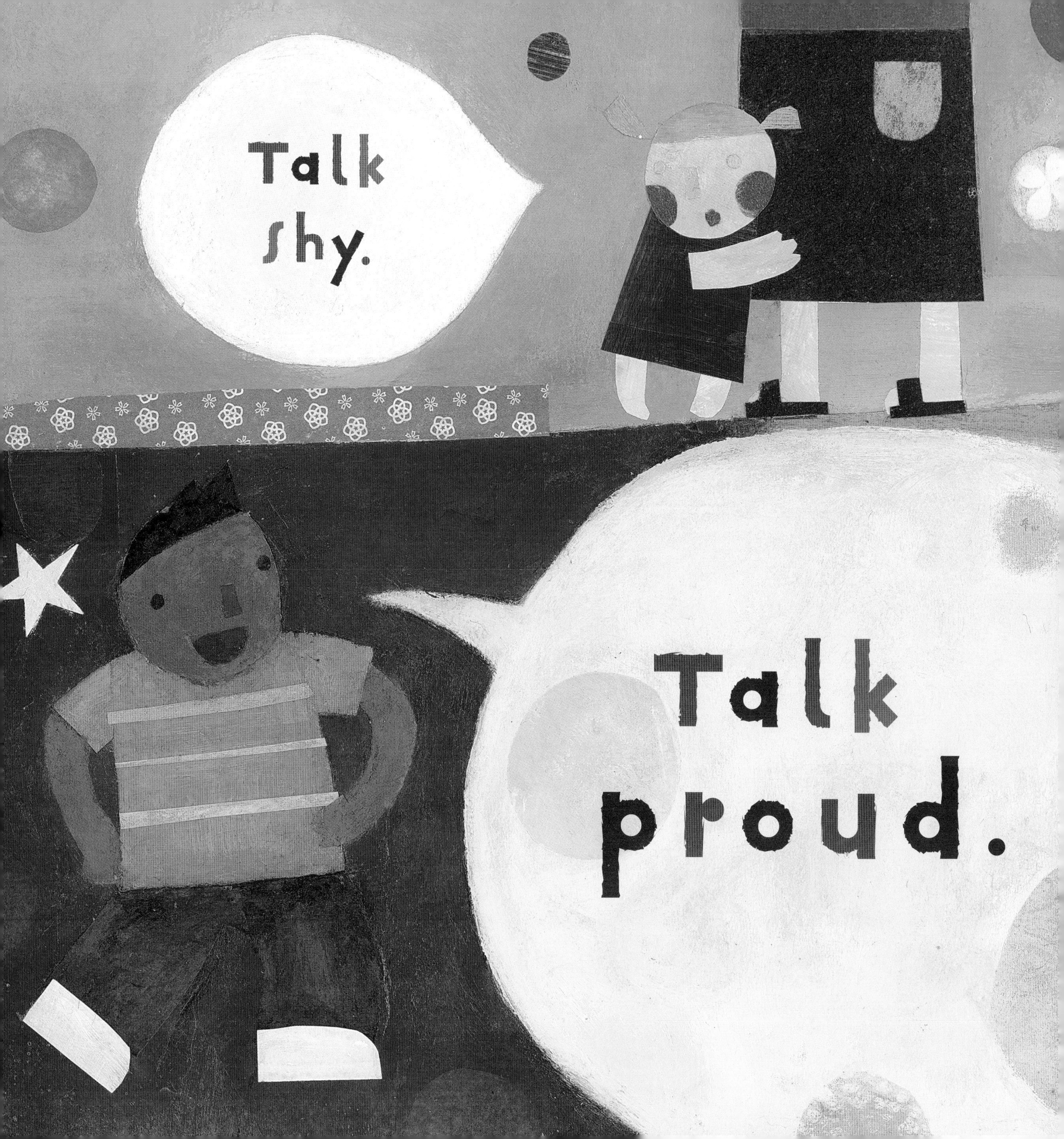
Talk shy.
Talk proud.

Talk high.

Talk low.

Way to go, talk peace.

In the air,
all around,

on the breeze,
in the trees.

On the street,
when you meet,

when you eat,

when you play.

In the day

or at night,
in the light of a dream,

talk peace.

Look at race

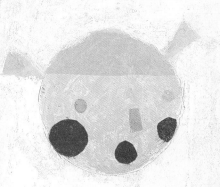

in the face,

anyplace,

anywhere,
don't scare,
talk peace.

Be alive,
gimme five.

When you party,
party jive.

Dance peace.

Talk peace.

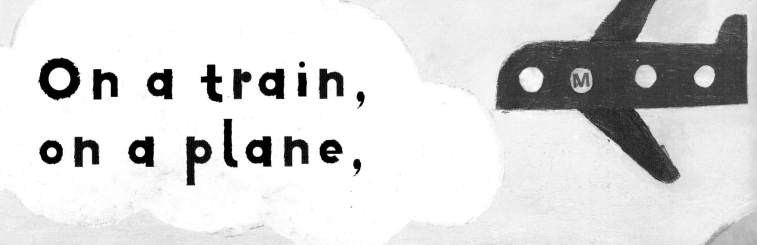

On a train,
on a plane,

in the sun, in the rain.

Understand

foreign land.

Take heart,
take part,

talk peace.

In a muddle,
when you huddle,

when you cuddle.

In a city, on the plain,

up the mountain, in the sea.

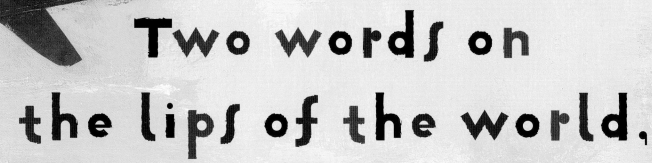

Two words on
the lips of the world,

talk peace.